Copyright © 2020 Clavis Publishing Inc., New York

Originally published as *Over de berg* in Belgium and the Netherlands by Clavis Uitgeverij, 2019
English translation from the Dutch by Clavis Publishing Inc., New York

Visit us on the Web at www.clavis-publishing.com.

Robin's Christmas Journey written and illustrated by Maya Onodera

ISBN 978-1-60537-577-9

This book was printed in July 2020 at Nikara, M. R. Štefánika 858/25, 963 01 Krupina, Slovakia.

First Edition
10 9 8 7 6 5 4 3 2 1

Robin's Christmas Journey

Maya Onodera

Clavis

NEW YORK

Christmas was just three days away, and Robin was about to head out on an adventure. He was off to visit his grandpa, who lived all the way on the other side of the mountain in the Valley of the Three Trees.

Robin knew it was going to be a difficult journey, but he was ready. He put some clothes and a gift for Grandpa in his backpack, he tucked his sleeping bag under his arm, and off he went.

A chilly wind blew as Robin began to walk uphill.
But Robin whistled cheerfully and kept close to the
mountain walls to avoid the wind.

Suddenly, a fierce gust of wind swept
Robin into the air.

He landed softly in a pile of leaves, but he was
back down at the bottom of the mountain.
And he had lost his sleeping bag!

Never mind, thought Robin as
he looked up at the mountain.
He wasn't going to give up so easily.
He stood up and began climbing again.

Robin climbed and climbed.
And the weather got
worse and worse.

Soon it started snowing, and
it was beginning to get dark.

Robin dug a bed in the snow and
used leaves to stay warm through the night.

Bright morning light awakened Robin.
The world was silent, covered by a white blanket of snow,
and the blue sky stretched over him.
Robin regained his courage and began to march.

Hooray! He finally reached
the top of the mountain.
Suddenly, Robin had an idea . . .
He knew how he could make up for
the time he had lost yesterday.

Robin looked for a tree and peeled off a piece of bark. And . . .

Ya-hoo!

Robin flew down the mountainside on his handmade snowboard.

Suddenly, a shadow whooshed overhead.

A falcon!

Robin had to get away
before he became the falcon's breakfast.

Robin made a giant leap and soared into the air
toward the protection of the forest.

Robin was safely hidden in the trees, but . . .

Crash!

Robin didn't see the branch
in front of him. Whoops.
The snowboard slipped out from under him
as his backpack got caught
on the branch.

Whoa . . . Robin began rolling down the hill.
And as he rolled he became a giant snowball.
The snowball grew *bigger* and *bigger* . . .
and he rolled faster and faster.

Eventually, he crashed at the bottom
of the hill. Everything went black.

When Robin woke up,
he felt cozy and warm.
There was a scent of sweetness in the air.
Where am I? he wondered.

Robin sat up and found three rabbits smiling down at him.
"Where am I?" Robin asked. "And who are you?"
"We found you in the snow and brought you to our den to warm up,"
the tallest rabbit said.
Robin thanked the rabbits and told them he was on his way to visit
his Grandpa in the Valley of the Three Trees for Christmas.

"Well, you'd better hurry up!" said the smallest rabbit. "Tomorrow is Christmas!"

"I've been sleeping for a whole day?" Robin asked. "How will I ever make it to the Valley of the Three Trees in time?"

"Well, there is one way," said the tallest rabbit. "Down the brook!"
"Down the brook?" Robin asked.
"Down the brook!" repeated all three rabbits together.

The three rabbits rushed into the kitchen. They came out with a small tin cup and a wooden spoon. "Now you can paddle down the brook that flows into the Valley of the Three Trees," the tallest rabbit said. They gave Robin some gingerbread and a map and sent him on his way.

Soon Robin heard the soft sound
of streaming water.

He didn't notice the cat that was
watching him from above.

Meow!

Oh no! Hurry, Robin!
Robin raced toward the brook.
When he saw the water down below,
he took a giant leap and . . .
landed safely in the water.

Before long, the water began to flow faster.
Robin found himself rushing down rapids.
His small boat rocked to and fro furiously,
but Robin held on.

Finally, the stream became calmer
and Robin saw the valley in the distance.
The sky turned pink.
The Three Trees came into sight.
Robin climbed ashore.

He no longer had his backpack with his present
for his grandfather. But he had this lovely boat!
It would make a nice gift! Robin was so excited
that he didn't notice he was being watched . . .

Suddenly, a fox appeared directly in front of him!
Robin froze with fear.
The fox jumped toward him.

Without giving it much thought, Robin broke the wooden
spoon in half and held the sharp ends toward the fox.
"Stay away!" Robin bravely shouted.

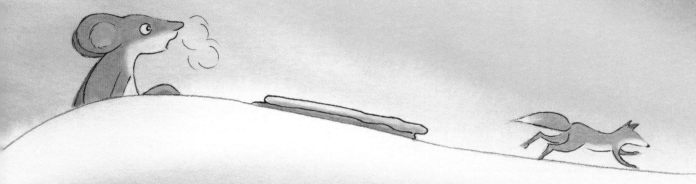

And lo and behold, it worked!
The fox turned and ran away.

Robin was so excited that he dropped the tin
cup boat and ran the rest of the way to
the Valley of the Three Trees.

"Grandpa! Grandpa!" Robin rushed through the door,
directly into the arms of his grandfather.

"Robin! I can't believe you are here.
Did you come here all alone?"

"Yes, I've been traveling for days.
But I'm so sorry, Grandpa," Robin cried,
"I lost your present along the way."

Grandpa held him close. "There is no better present in the whole world than **you!**"